for North Avenue Beach

Copyright © 2006 by Elisha Cooper ◆ All rights reserved. ◆ Published by Orchard Books, an imprint of Scholastic Inc., *Publishers since 1920.*

ORCHARD BOOKS and design are registered trademarks of Watts Publishing Group, Ltd., used under license.

SCHOLASTIC and associated logos are trademarks and/or registered trademarks of Scholastic Inc. No part of this publication

may be reproduced, stored in a retrieval system, or transmitted in any form or by any means, electronic, mechanical, photocopying,

recording, or otherwise, without written permission of the publisher.

For information regarding permission, write to Orchard Books, Scholastic Inc., Permissions Department, 557 Broadway, New York, NY 10012.

Library of Congress Cataloging-in-Publication Data: Cooper, Elisha. Beach / Elisha Cooper p. cm. Summary: Women, men, boys, and girls spend

a day at the beach enjoying a variety of activities on the sand and in the water. [1. Beaches—Fiction. 2. Seashore—Fiction.] I. Title.

PZ7.C784737Bea 2006 [E]—dc22 2005020195 ISBN-13: 978-0-439-68785-0 ◆ ISBN-10: 0-439-68785-3

10 9 8 7   14 15 16

Printed in Malaysia 108 ◆ Reinforced Binding for Library Use

First edition, June 2006 ◆ The text type was set in 16-point Shannon. The display type was set in Linotype Pisa.

Watercolor and pencil were used for the illustrations in this book. Book design by Alison Klapthor

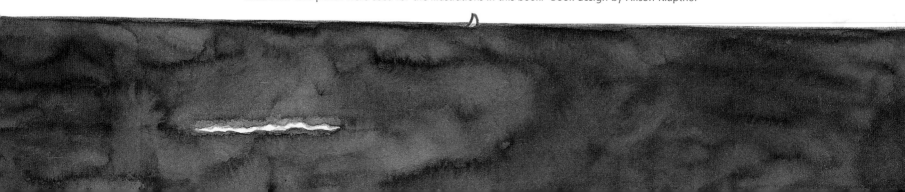

Elisha Cooper

BEACH

Orchard Books ◆ New York ◆ an imprint of Scholastic Inc.

way to the beach! Away to sand and salt water, to rolling dunes and pounding waves. Away to swimsuits and sunscreen, to lying on towels and listening to the sound of the ocean. As the day begins, the beach is empty, waiting to be filled.

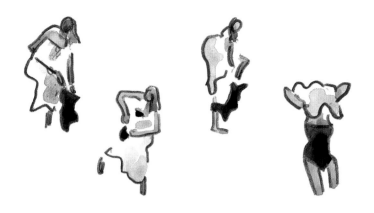

A woman changes into her swimsuit under her towel.

Another woman spreads her towel on the sand.

The wind is not helping a man put up his umbrella.

A woman pushes and pulls a packed wagon.

Parents yell, "*Don't forget sunscreen!*" before their children run away.

A woman lathers on sunscreen and reaches for the spot that cannot be reached.

Two sisters fill buckets with sand
and start building a sculpture.

A couple of boys drip
a sand castle.

A boy and a girl ride their
parents in a crab race.

Another girl covers a friend
up to his neck in sand.

The only person in pants is
flying a kite high overhead.

Seagulls watch everything,
hovering until made to move.

Some people jump into the water with a shout.

Some wade in an inch . . . at . . . a . . . time.

Some go in and forget
they are wearing glasses.

Some are thrown in.

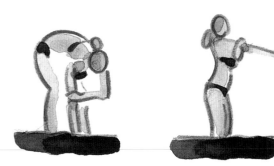

Some wash their arms at the water's edge,
then go back to shore.

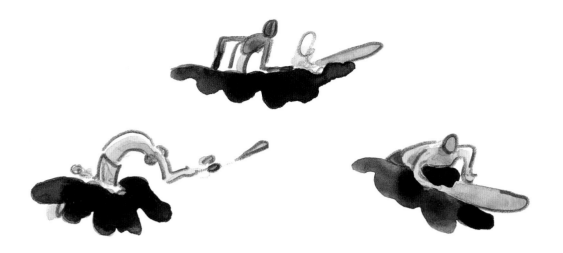

Some push into the waves with boards.

Some launch kayaks.

A few don't come out
until the end of the day,

and some don't go in at all.

Sunbathers lie side by side — flicking sand, swatting flies, dabbing sweat, turning pages, flipping from their fronts to their backs. Above the sunbathers is the lifeguard chair and the lifeguard looking out at the water.

A boy pretends he's a sea turtle and lets the waves carry him out.

A woman inflates an inner tube, but only goes in up to her ankles.

Two girls sift wet sand through their fingers and talk.

Other girls fill buckets with water and try not to get wet.

A group of sandpipers rush in and out with the waves.

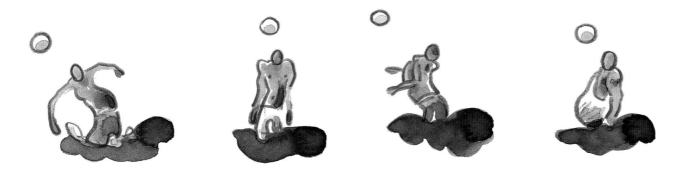

Friends juggle a soccer ball with their heads.

A dog barks at waves, then retrieves a piece of driftwood.

A man wades with his baby, keeping an eye out for jellyfish.

Couples climb on each other's shoulders and try to knock each other off.

A wave takes a boy under before tossing him back to shore.

The waves come in hills and valleys,

in mountains and canyons,

in craggy peaks

and sweeping plains.

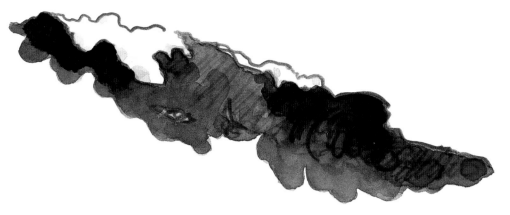

They come in boisterous and loud

and they leave with a quiet pull.

Waves are nature's roller coaster.

The perfect wave lifts high and drops low,
and can be felt in the stomach.

There's the roar of a motorboat, the slap of its bottom against the water.

There's the whine of Jet Skis skipping over the surface.

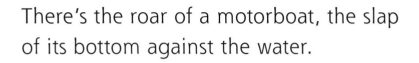

There's a rowboat the size of a bathtub.

There's the ruffle of sails from a sailboat tacking in the wind.

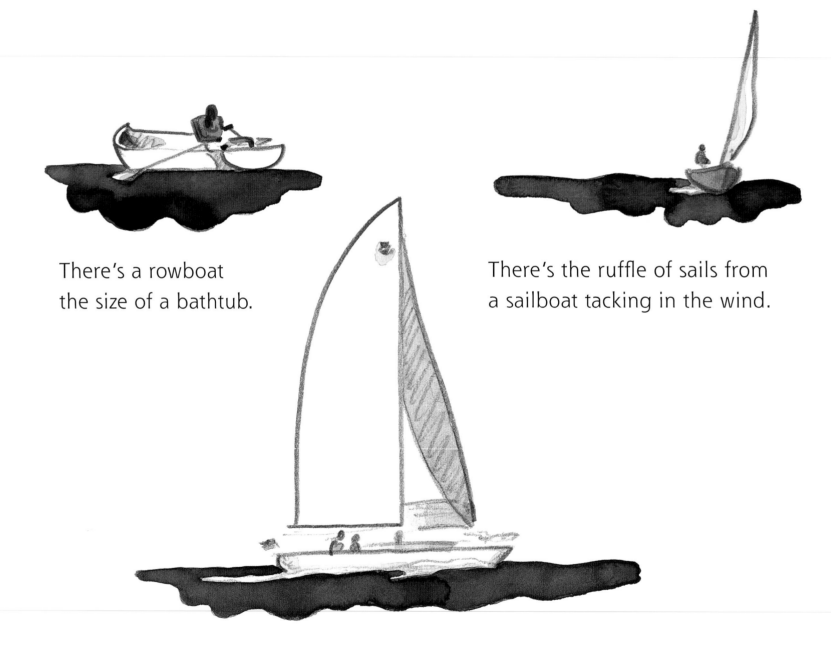

There's the boom of a sail filling on a larger sailboat.

There's the drone of an airplane dragging a tail banner.

There's no sound from the old man and the sea kayak.

There's the *thump-thump-thump* of a coast guard helicopter.

There's the muffled clanging of the bell on a distant buoy.

Sound underwater is softened, sloshing and gurgling.

Picnic baskets open with peanut-butter-and-jelly sandwiches, peaches, cookies, and iced tea. Towels get sticky. After lunch, children walk past the outdoor showers to the truck that sells ice-cream sandwiches.

The smell of grilling mixes with the smell of the ocean.
A baseball game plays on a radio as seagulls circle overhead.
Nearby rocks are covered with broken crab legs, shells,
mussels, ladybugs, barnacles, and seaweed that looks like lettuce.

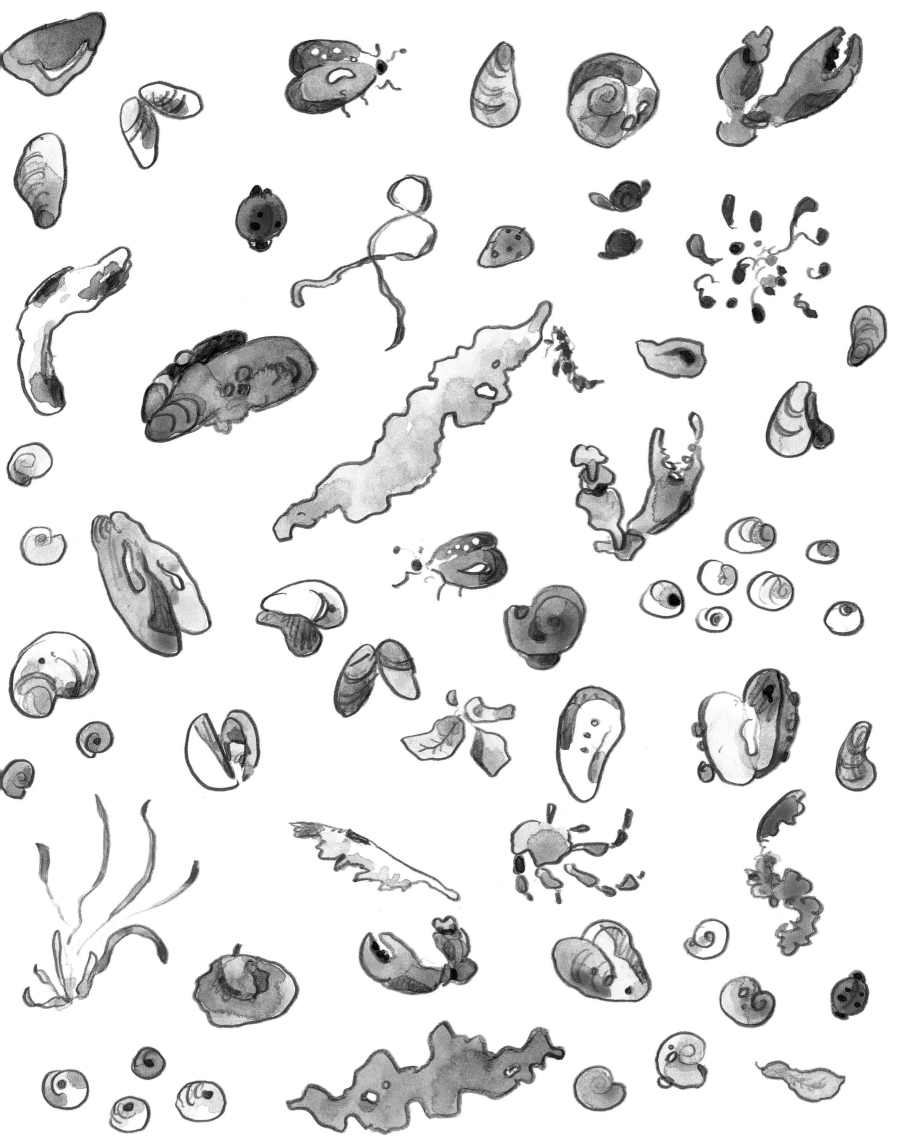

Behind the beach is a marsh, quiet and still. Hidden in the marsh are egrets staring into the water, ospreys sitting on nests, and butterflies flitting over the tops of reeds.

At one end of the beach is a rock point and a lighthouse. The lighthouse looks out at the ocean. Rocks the size of trucks slope into the water. Waves crash into them and jump into the air.

Clouds scatter across the sky, changing shape as they go.

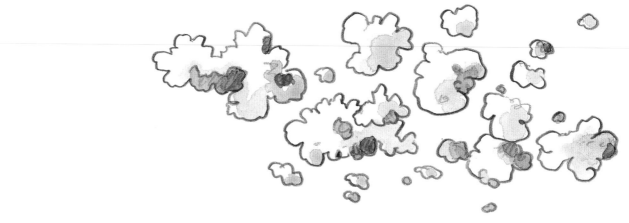

These clouds are spilled popcorn,

these clouds are sheep,

and these clouds are waves.

This cloud is a whale eating a pancake.

This cloud is the shape of Alaska,   no, Hawaii.

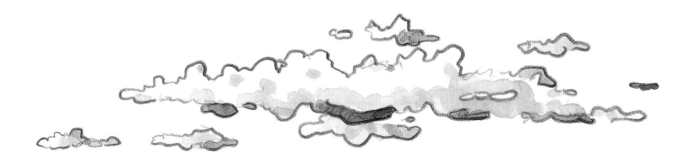

The clouds race one another from one end of the beach to the other.

A woman changes out of her swimsuit under her towel.

Another woman shakes out her towel and folds it up.

The wind helps close an umbrella.

A woman gathers her belongings and packs her wagon.

Parents yell, "*Don't forget . . .*" but their voices are carried away by the wind.

The effects of sunscreen are revealed.

Two sisters finish their sculpture,
and one signs her name with her toe.

A man searches for lost things
in the sand.

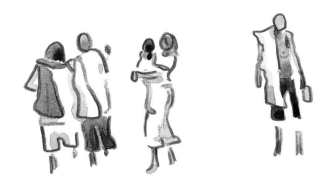

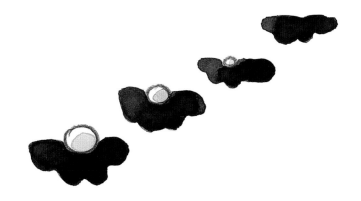

Someone points out at the water
and everyone looks: *porpoises!*

A ball floats out to sea, smaller
and smaller, and then it disappears.

A group of girls wrap themselves
in towels.

Seagulls pull their heads tight into their
shoulders and watch everyone leave.

As the sun sets and the clouds change color, the beach empties. A last jump in the water, another last jump. Then up the sand and over the dunes with a stop at the outdoor shower. Sand is everywhere — between toes and in bathing suits and inside ears. Inside, too, is the motion of the waves, the knowledge of a day well spent, a day to remember when the beach is far away.